I0659732

Slub Glub in the Weird World of the Weeping Willows

by A. Goldfarb

SPUNK GOBLIN PRESS

SPUNK GOBLIN PRESS
AN IMPRINT OF ERASERHEAD PRESS

ERASERHEAD PRESS
205 NE BRYANT
PORTLAND, OR 97211

WWW.ERASERHEADPRESS.COM

ISBN: 1-933929-87-1

Copyright © 2009 by Andrew Goldfarb

All rights reserved. No part of this book may be reproduced or transmitted in any form or by any means, electronic or mechanical, including photocopying, recording, or by any information storage and retrieval system, without the written consent of the publisher, except where permitted by law.

Printed in the USA.

Slub Glub in the Weird World of the Weeping Willows

by A. Goldfarb

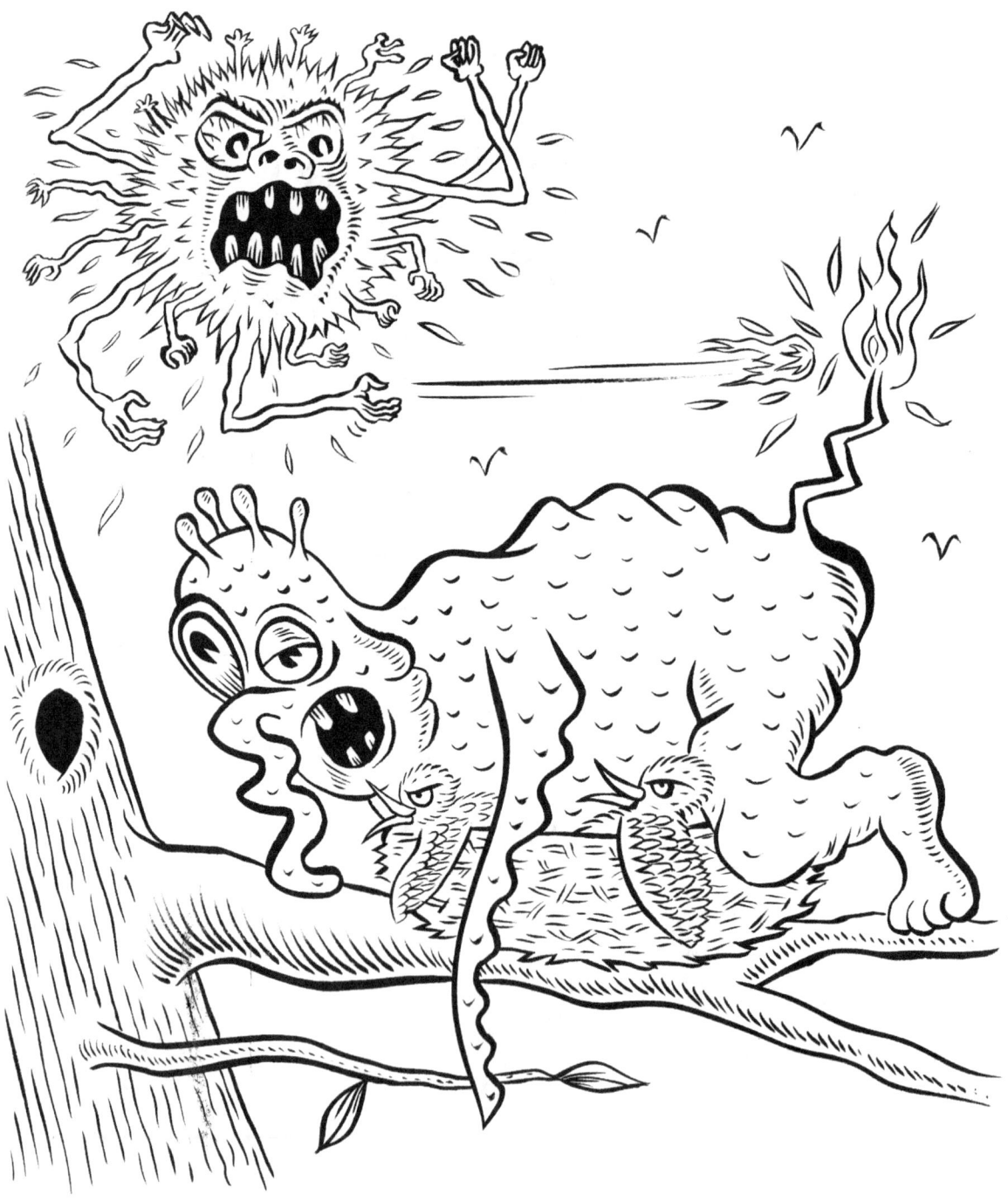

Chapter One

The Hideous Shrieking
of the Rising Sun

On Tuesday of last week, Slub Glub was awoken from his peaceful slumbers by the hideous shrieking of the rising Sun. "Get up!" the fiery orb yelled, as she did every day, sending flaming embers in the general direction of Slub Glub's blue, globular body.

Slub Glub raised one of his two tentacles to cover his ear holes, ignoring the star's hysterical screaming. In response, the Sun wound up one of its thousand angry fists and pitched a blazing comet down, setting Slub Glub's tail on fire.

With a murmur of discontent, Slub Glub rolled over onto his belly, sniffing the acrid smoke that was now coming from his bottom. Emerging unwillingly from behind the veil of sleep, he opened his lazy yellow eyes and saw that he was on fire. With a snort from his dangling trunk he briefly roused his bulbous head in alarm, but his yelp became a yawn, and Slub Glub

decided to ignore his flaming tail and attempted to go back to sleep, burying his face in one tentacle and hoping to get a fresh start under better (and less fiery) circumstances a few hours later, or even the next day.

6

However, within moments his repose was again disturbed, this time by a violent pecking against where his belly button would have been, if he had had one. A muffled "Squawk" emerged from the same region, and then with a concerted effort, the family of birds who had been uncomfortably squished beneath Slub Glub's flabby, flatulent body managed to forcibly eject him from their nest. Apparently he had been using their home as a bed, and was very much an uninvited guest. Landing on a mound of dirt, Slub Glub was forced to greet the new day, and found himself eye to eye with an earthworm.

Chapter Two

The Worm's-Eye View

"Hmmph. Watch where you flop there, fatty," said the disagreeable worm.

"It's not my fault. I've been evicted," said Slub Glub, getting up and dusting himself off, rubbing his lumpy torso with his two tentacles. "There's a housing crisis, you know."

"I wouldn't know," the unpleasant worm replied, burrowing back into his mound of dirt. Slub Glub sat alone for a few minutes, until a distinct rumbling in his belly disturbed the silence. Suddenly hungry, he poked his head into the earthworm's mound of dirt and felt around for the nasty little grub with his tongue. Successful, he swallowed the earthworm, only to find that the earthworm was aptly named in that he did indeed taste like earth, and not good earth at that.

"Let me out," the undigested worm yelled from inside Slub Glub's mouth, pounding his forehead against a cheek. Slub Glub obligingly spit him out

back onto the ground.

"That was rude," said the worm.

"Look who's talking!"

"If you're hungry, why don't you go down the hill and find yourself some coconuts," the worm said with finality, diving back down his hole in the ground, this time taking care to plug the opening behind him.

8

"Coconuts?" mused Slub Glub, who wasn't sure what those were but liked cocoa and liked nuts, and figured the combination of the two would be a good way to turn the day around. He raised himself onto his two floppy blue feet and began to waddle earnestly downhill, commencing a journey that would take him through the forest, to the bottom of the deepest sea, into the farthest regions of space, then face to face with The Cosmic Powers That Be, and eventually to another world entirely, all before dinner-time.

Chapter Three

Too Many Teeth

Slub Glub slid downhill fast, bumping right into the coconut tree that he was searching for, and in doing so managed to dislodge a coconut from beneath one of its giant fronds. The coconut fell directly down onto Slub Glub's soft noggin, but luckily for him his head had four knob-like protuberances jutting out on top, which proved perfect for the catching of a falling coconut, thereby protecting Slub Glub from a brain-crushing blow.

He grabbed the fruit from atop his head and stuffed it into his mouth, gnashing his four yellow teeth in an attempt to chew through the fruit's brown furry shell. Then, for the second time that morning, he experienced a searing pain in his rear end.

Wriggling around to take a better look, Slub Glub was dismayed to find that a shark was attached to his tail. Its many pointy teeth were deeply immersed in Slub Glub's dangling prehensile appendage.

"That's curious, I didn't know you fishy types got

all the way out here," Slub Glub remarked to the shark that was trying to eat him.

"What's that supposed to mean?" the shark retorted.

"I mean, I thought you stayed in the water mostly."

"I am in the water," said the shark, and Slub Glub saw that this was so—he was up to his tentacles in murky, muddy fluid, which extended for as far as he could see.

"How did this happen?" asked Slub Glub, expecting the shark to have all the answers.

11

"Danged if I know. Global warming, maybe." The shark spit out Slub Glub's tail with a grimace. "You taste terrible," he said, swimming away.

Not being much of a swimmer himself, Slub Glub wrapped his tentacles around the coconut tree and inched his way upward. Once at the top, he peered out at the swampified forest, trying to figure out how it got so wet all of a sudden.

Chapter Four

Sad and Salty Streams

12

From his treetop Slub Glub saw a mass of weeping willow trees crying hysterically; their overflowing tears appeared to be the cause of the recent deluge. A group of about a dozen were clustered together, swaying back and forth and emitting piteous wails, their plumes of cascading branches shuddering as they shed great gobs of teardrops from their green leaves.

Slub Glub climbed down from his coconut perch and swam downstream to where the willows were gathered. "My dear trees, you've got to stop this sobbing," Slub Glub implored the inconsolable willows.

"Whaaaugh," was their reply, as they continued blubbering.

"Why on earth are you so upset? Your crying is making a flood and we're all getting much wetter than we'd care to."

"We're going bald," replied the tallest of the trees.

Slub Glub looked up. "You seem to have plenty of leaves up there."

Slub Glub in the Weird World of the Weeping Willows

"No, they're all being eaten," the tree replied, and with that the other willows began weeping and wailing even louder. "Look," he said, holding out one of his branches, which indeed seemed to have been the victim of recent nibbling; a number of the leaves had noticeable bite marks, and the end of the branch seemed to have been chewed to a nub.

"Ah, I know what that's like. A shark was trying to eat me just a moment ago… Which is why we can't have this many tears, you've upset the whole forest here, we're awash in your misery and we're not used to such streams of sadness puddling up our grasses." "Don't blame us, blame those bark-biting thieves in black masks that come around every night," said the weeping willow, his foliage drooping in for-saken fashion.

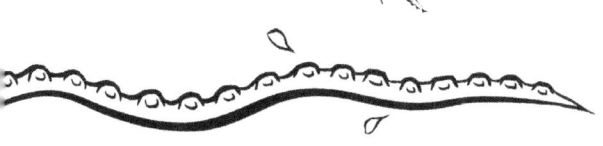

Chapter Five

In Search of Wayward Raccoons

"Thieves?" Slub Glub queried.

"Furry thieves on four legs! That's who's making us cry," one of the willow trees moaned, and the other trees joined in with more piteous wailing. The youngest female willow tree screamed especially loud.

"There's one still in my hair," she yelled, shaking her willowy branches furiously, flinging a sinister-looking raccoon to the ground. The other trees recoiled in fear. The raccoon, still munching on a leaf from the tree, hissed menacingly at Slub Glub and the petrified trees, then bounded off into the distance.

"Alas! These fuzzy demons will be the death of us! Without our glorious foliage, we will die of naked shame!" the tallest willow wailed, tears once again raining down onto the swampy soil.

"Stop!" Slub Glub cried, fearing that a renewed outburst of crying would carry him out to sea. "Dry your sappy tear ducts, I will follow this crooked creature to

his lair, and convince he and his gang to cease feeding on your fragile foliage."

"I'll come with you," said the young tree who had flung out the raccoon.

"Good idea," said Slub Glub, extending a tentacle. "Slub Glub is the name."

"I'm Willowmina. Pleased to meet you," the tree replied, and with one of her branches shook Slub Glub's tentacle. She bade goodbye to her fellow weeping willows in the grove and then the two of them traipsed down the soggy hill and into the shadows beyond.

15

Chapter Six

Masked Marauders Amassed

16

After a short trek, Slub Glub and Willowmina came to a marshy area alongside a muddy stream.

"There's those blasted bandits," Willowmina spat, pointing one branch towards a hollow log, from which a couple of bushy tails poked out. Slub Glub stuck his long, curly nose inside and snorted loudly.

"Hey! We're sleeping in here!" grumbled one of the raccoons from inside the log.

"Hmmmph," Willowmina muttered, rolling the log over with one of her root-feet. Three raccoons tumbled out of the hollow tree-trunk.

"What's the big idea?" one of them asked, looking up to the willow tree and then over at Slub Glub.

Willowmina adopted a chiding tone. "Oh, so it's okay for you to hang out in our hair all night chewing on our leaves, but as soon as we disturb your beauty rest, then heaven help us."

18

The raccoons fell silent; surprise and then embarrassment registered on their faces. The black masks around their eyes made them look even guiltier.

"Oooh, right, about that. Um... You're one of those willow trees from up the hill?" one of the raccoons asked.

"Yes, and my whole family is up there weeping wildly, their foliage falling out from all your rustling! Why can't you spend the night down here in these hollow logs, instead of bothering us?"

The three raccoons looked at each other and then back at Willowmina. Slub Glub, meanwhile, had gotten his nose stuck inside the log and was struggling futilely to free himself. "We're sorry," the raccoons said in unison, and then the largest among them continued, "but it's not our fault. We only climb on you and the other willow trees to get away from the evil grinning devils, who laugh at us in cruel mockery. And then while we're up in your branches hiding from them, we get awful hungry and there's nothing to eat but your leaves."

Willowmina stared at the raccoons, unsure how to react. Slub Glub had finally gotten his nose free and he approached the group. "Devils? What devils" he asked.

"Hyena devils!" the raccoons shuddered together.

Chapter Seven

What Witches Ride

19

Willowmina put one of her branches to her head, and with great exasperation, said, "Hyenas. Fine. If we can get them to stop laughing at you and calling you names, will you then quit climbing up our trunks at night and chewing on us?" The three raccoons nodded eagerly. "Okay, then. Where are these hyenas at?"

"They only come out at night."

In short order a decision was reached, that Willowmina and Slub Glub would stay with the raccoons into the evening, until the hyenas came around. Slub Glub, who still felt that he had been cheated out of his slumber by the rising sun, climbed back into the hollow log with the raccoons and began snoring loudly. Willowmina sat down next to them, folding her branches together and drooping her fragrant foliage onto the boggy earth.

Hours slithered slowly past, until finally the big angry sun in the sky descended, flailing his thousand arms as the world dipped once more into darkness.

Slub Glub in the Weird World of the Weeping Willows

Then soon after, the silence of the forest was pierced with a chorus of cackling laughter. Hearing the hysterical hyenas in the distance, the raccoons awoke with a start. Slub Glub crawled out of the log, and instantly wished that he hadn't.

Streaming out of the darkness came a dozen spotted hyenas, their toothy maws twisted into great clownish grimaces. With a bear-like gait they approached, and one of the sleek, fanged creatures leaned towards Slub Glub, making an awful kind of laughing sound in his direction.

"Bwah-ha-ha!" the hyena taunted.

Slub Glub couldn't take such abuse, and he climbed up Willowmina's trunk to get away from the nasty animal. Willowmina, being significantly taller, had a different perspective. From where she stood she could see that the hyenas, all twelve of them, were not alone—on the back of each was a witch, and each witch was carrying a torch.

With a long sweeping swipe from her biggest branch, Willowmina knocked the twelve witches off their hyenas, and the horrid hags fell down onto the ground.

Chapter Eight

Buttery Shudders

"A pox on you!" cackled one of the witches. Her green nose was spotted with warts, and a pointed black hat covered her stringy grey hair. She and her coven of eleven other sorceresses were rubbing their bottoms and moaning, still smarting from being smacked down. The hyenas, having now had their wicked riders removed, became calm and docile and stared blankly into space. Seeing that the situation was now under control, Slub Glub and the three raccoons came down from their hiding place among Willowmina's branches.

"I thought you witchy women all rode on broomsticks," Slub Glub commented.

"I'll turn you into a toad!" cackled the hag. "By the dust of mummies and the crust in tummies, with fang and claw and tooth and awe, I call down thunder and cast you under, a spell to render you a frog, you hog!" The witch waved her torch aloft with great dramatic intent, but the fire on it had gone out, which apparently

diminished her hex-casting techniques. "Um, just a moment," she muttered embarrassedly, and she reached over to one of the hyenas' hindquarters.

24

Slub Glub discreetly moved away from the witch and sidled up to a hyena sitting somewhat distant from the rest of the group. "Hyena, tell me, what is that crazy crone doing?"

"Oh, she's getting some butter from under that hyena. These witches have been using our butter to light their torches."

"I didn't know hyenas made butter. Are you related to cows?"

"No, any creature can make butter if they try hard enough. We use it to mark our territory, or at least we did, until these loathsome ladies started stealing it all from us. Then they light their torches and ride around on top of us all night, using their fiendish sorcery to make us hysterical and mean."

"Why would they want to do that?"

"You'd have to ask them."

Chapter Nine

Evil Words are Spoken

Slub Glub came back to the coven of witches, who had now gathered around Willowmina and were trying to set fire to her with their torches, which had somehow been relit with the hyena butter. Willowmina blew the torches out by waving her branches around, which had the beneficial side effect of knocking the witches down again. Slub Glub walked over to the witch that had tried to turn him into a toad.

"Tell me, mystic lady, why are you riding around on these hyenas, and why are you hypnotizing them into laughing at everyone?"

"Goblin! I'll banish you to the nether realms!" was her reply, and she pulled a gnarled old wooden wand from inside her natty dress. Waving it wildly towards Slub Glub, she recited this incantation:

Oh putridious fumescense and mottled bottles,
I doom your bones to dry rot and potholes!
The night is a mouth that will swallow you whole

Leaving you shiftless and fruitless in bowl.
Lichen and fungus will grow on your surface
Good riddance to you, oh blue shaded bug face~

26

Slub Glub liked the poem, and did a bit of a jig while she was reciting it, but didn't feel particularly banished, and was starting to lose interest in the situation when the hyena that he had been talking to earlier spoke up.

"I think the reason they're riding us around at night and having us make such a ruckus is that they're trying to scare away the ghosts."

"Oh, that makes sense," Slub Glub replied.

Chapter Ten

A Multitude
of Mysteries

"The heads of a hundred horses will be lodged in your cheek, you freak!" The witch was still trying to cast a spell on Slub Glub. "With my fourth eye I espy your feet festooned with flies!"

"Be careful, Lumprella, remember what happened last time," said a second witch, gesturing for the head hag Lumprella, the queen of the cackling crones, to stop her hoodoo-ing.

"What happened last time?" Slub Glub asked. The witches glanced at each other, but were mum on the subject. Then one of the hyenas ventured forth.

"They think their witchery has raised the spirits of the dead, and now phantoms are following them, seeking revenge for the disturbance of their rest," the hyena said.

"I know how they feel," Slub Glub replied.

28

Lumprella broke down into confessional crowing. "It's true! Our incantations have awakened the restless souls of the deceased! Our spells are too strong! Our hexes are too effective! Too black in their blackedness and magical in their magicality! The doorways of the doomed have flung open and hideous apparitions from beyond the grave now haunt our waking moments... Soon they will catch up to us and drag us back to their bleak and barren land! That is why we must light our torches with butter from hyena bottoms and ride these creatures though the woods, their hyena mockery reverberating through the shrubbery as we mesmerize their mammal minds, manipulating their mandibles to laugh at all in the night. What else can we do? What else can prevent these ghosts from feeding upon our bones and boiling us in our own brewed stew?"

Willowmina pondered this explanation a moment, and then commented back that this all sounded very complicated and perhaps these ghosts that they were running from were really just fireflies.

Chapter Eleven

Specters Spectacular

"Just fireflies?" Lumprella shrieked. "See for yourself! They are upon us!" All the witches screamed and ran for the hills, and the hyenas and raccoons followed suit. Slub Glub and Willowmina stared into the darkness, but didn't see anything.

"Do you see anything?" asked Willowmina.

"No, but my ears do," said Slub Glub, listening to the faint sound of drums in the distance, which were playing a helter-skelter rhythm. Slub Glub began to dance. Willowmina put her branches to the ground to better pick up the vibrations, and as the strange beat got louder she started to shake, her leaves fluttering in the yellow moonlight. Then the first apparition appeared.

A disheveled man in a striped shirt appeared, dragging his limbs behind him. He was semi-translucent, emitting a faint greenish glow. The weeds and rocks were

32

visible through his pale torso. He wore a cap and one eyeball was dangling from his head. It looked like it had been a long time since he was alive. "Wuuuuuuugh," he moaned, approaching Slub Glub and Willowmina, who stopped moving and stared back at him and his drooping orb.

"Let me get that for you," Willowmina said, poking his eyeball back into its socket with one of her branches. Instead of being grateful, the phantom became irate, flailing his ghostly arms and emitting a mournful howl. "Well, never mind then," Willowmina said. The striped once-was-a-man looked back towards the darkness, and soon a whole motley crew of broken-down specters appeared, all in various states of decay, and all of a see-through green composition. They muttered and shambled, dragging their bones behind them, slowly scraping past Willowmina and Slub Glub.

"Hey, the witches went the other way," Willowmina called after the last of the crusty derelicts.

"Witches?" said the shadowy man, seemingly confused.

"Aren't you chasing after the witches who conjured you from your graves with their spells?"

"No, we're not after any witches, we're just going where the Baron tells us to," he answered, and shuffled on.

Slub Glub and Willowmina stared at each other. "The Baron?" they both repeated aloud, wondering...

Chapter Twelve

A Well Dressed Man in the Woods

33

"That would be me," said a voice out of the darkness. A glowing red ember slowly radiated outwards, attached to a cigar being smoked by a tall man in a top hat. His face was painted a deathly white on top of his dark skin, an effect made even more morbid by a set of rib-bones that were tattooed on his torso, which was partially covered by a tattered tuxedo. This formal attire was complimented by a large walking stick, which hissed at Slub Glub and Willowmina, as it was actually a snake. The tails of his coat were adorned with feathers and a number of crosses and hearts scrawled in chalk. A conga drum was at his side. Evidently it was he that had provided the ghostly rhythms that they heard earlier.

The Baron came up close to the willow tree and the little blue mutant. "But I don't know who you are,"

he said with a large smile, revealing a few teeth made of gold and a few that were missing. He stubbed out his cigar and put his head close to Willowmina's trunk. "But let me guess." He breathed deeply, then stared deep into the willow tree's foliage. "You, my dear girl, are a young sapling, of the powerful and wise weeping willow variety, who has recently encountered some friends of mine who have lost their way." Despite his jovial tone, Willowmina was scared of this unusual gentleman.

35

He then squatted down and inspected Slub Glub. "And you, my little blue friend, are a thing that should not be; a creature born of chemical wastes and strange breeding." He took one of Slub Glub's tentacles in his large hand, each finger of which was adorned with a ring, some of diamonds, some of tin. "I am pleased to know you." His breath smelled of cemetery dust and fish, which Slub Glub found pleasant.

"Now tell me," the Baron said, rising to his feet and addressing them both, "exactly what was it that you were saying to my men?"

Chapter Thirteen

Explanations Are Offered

36

"I was asking those ghosts if they were chasing after the witches," Willowmina explained.

"Now why would they be chasing after witches, and how is it your concern," he slowly drawled, as he took a decanter and glass from inside his top hat and poured himself a drink. The liquid was a misty amber color, and small clouds seemed to gather above it. He stirred it with the tail of his snake.

Willowmina took a deep breath, and then replied, "There's a coven of witches in this wood that believe that their spell-casting and hex-making and general witchery has somehow awakened the dead from their graves, and those restless dead are the ghosts who just passed by. The reason we care is that in order to keep these ghosts at bay, the witches have taken to riding on

hyenas and hypnotizing the animals into laughing and shrieking, figuring that this would scare the ghosts away. The problem with that is that these hyena hysterics have had an unfortunate effect on the raccoon population; the raccoons become anxious and afraid, and take refuge in the branches of the weeping willow trees, such as myself, and while immersed in our green boughs they nibble on our leaves out of hunger."

38

She waved a branch with tattered leaves in the Baron's face to prove her point. The Baron took her branch in his hand and took a close look with his eye and a deep whiff with his nose, which was pierced with an iron ring turned red with rust. "Yes, I do see what you mean."

Slub Glub tugged on the Baron's pants-leg, eager to contribute his part of the story. "And then when the willows get all bitten, they start crying a great deal, which starts a great flood, reaching all the way to the ocean, and then sharks get carried in and start eating my tail when I'm trying to have breakfast."

"I see," mused the Baron thoughtfully.

Chapter Fourteen

Shepherd of Souls

The Baron tossed the last swallow from his glass and crushed it beneath his feet. Then he lackadaisically pulled a cigar from his pocket and lit it with a small flame he got from rubbing his fingertips together. He took a drag and addressed his two new acquaintances with a toothy grin and a gleam in his eye. "Well, that's an awful lot of he-did-this-so-she-did-that."

Willowmina had an uneasy feeling, and tried to hurry things along. "All we want to do is keep those ghosts from following the witches."

"Ah, yes, then all your troubles would... Cease. Well, I will tell you where those 'ghosts,' as you call them, are going." The Baron draped his snake around his neck and spread his hands wide. "I am known to some as Baron Samedi, and to some as Baron Saturday, and to others not at all. I know more than this world contains, and it is my job to see that all who are no longer of this earth find their way to Guinee." As he

spoke the moon shone brighter in the sky, bathing the night forest in a pale greenish light. Dark clouds crept from behind the hills and a mist gathered in the air.

"Guinee?" asked Willomina.

"Guinee is another land, very far from here, and not in this realm. It is where the dearly departed belong, and it is I that sends them there. That is where these phantoms are en route to now, and I am their guide. Now do you understand, little tree?"

"Sort of. But would you mind sending these ghosts through another forest?" Willowmina asked, and the moon suddenly went dark and the black clouds broke, sending torrents of rain pouring down upon them. Slub Glub dove into a mud puddle and buried his head, fearing that Willomina had made the formidable Baron angry. Willowmina stood her ground, as she believed her request to be reasonable.

"Hahahahahahahahahahahahahahahaahha," Baron Samedi exclaimed, beside himself with laughter. He slapped his knees.

Chapter Fifteen

A Drink Beneath Black Skies

"What's so funny?" Willowmina asked.

"Every forest is forever full of ghosts... Every forest and every city and every desert," the Baron chuckled. Then he saw how crestfallen Willowmina was, and whether it was out of pity, or as a prank, he offered a ray of hope to her. "I tell you what, though, little tree. These specters that have been parading as of late, and creating all this witch-hyena-raccoon whatnot, have all been floating in on this stream, which is where I meet up with them every midnight." He pointed a bony finger to the craggy creek that ran along the forest to their left, where a modest ripple of dirty water gurgled softly. "If you follow this stream back to where it starts, maybe you can discover why these poor souls are being sent down this way, and try to stop it, hmmm?"

Willomina brightened at this possibility. "Thank you," she said hastily, and reached down to pull Slub Glub out of the mud.

Baron Samedi produced another glass from beneath

his hat, and pulling a flask from his pocket, he poured himself another drink. "My pleasure, sweet flower. But what's the hurry? Why don't you both stay and have a drink with me."

Slub Glub, emerging from his hiding place with a face covered in black dirt, thought this was a fine invitation and reached for the glass with his tentacle, but Willowmina pulled him away by the nose toward the creek bed. "Thank you very much, sir, but we really must be going, we want to get to the bottom of this as soon as possible."

The Baron seemed to find this highly amusing, and laughed again. "Oh, I wish you luck with that, getting to the bottom of it. Maybe you'll even find the top!" And with that he wandered back into the darkness, in the direction of the poor souls he shepherded, chuckling to himself and puffing on his cigar.

43

Chapter Sixteen

Weary Waters of the Sad Stream

44

Slub Glub and Willowmina stood at the edge of the stream and pondered their next move. "It doesn't look very deep," Willowmina said.

"I don't think I can swim," Slub Glub mused.

"Me neither," said Willowmina.

"Yes, you can," came a voice out of nowhere, sounding none too enthusiastic.

"Who said that?" Willowmina asked, looking around.

"Down here, in the water," the voice replied.

Slub Glub got down on his knees and stared into the muddy creek. "Are you a fish?" he asked.

"No," the voice replied with a sigh. "I'm a babbling brook."

"Oh," said Willowmina, "and how do you know I can swim?"

Slub Glub in the Weird World
of the Weeping Willows

"You're a tree," the brook replied, as if Willowmina and Slub Glub were the stupidest critters it had ever encountered. "Trees can float. Just get in, and I'll carry you along, everyone does it these days," he said, sounding put-upon.

"Well, not if you're going to be grumpy about it," Willowmina replied.

"Oh, just get in, after all these glowing sailors with their drooping limbs it'll be a change of pace."

"Glowing sailors?" asked Willomina. "Those must be the ghosts that just passed by. You know where they're coming from?"

The brook sighed again. "Yes, of course I do, they've been floating on me for weeks now, get in and I'll take you to the ocean from whence they appear."

Willowmina put one root in the muddy water daintily and shivered a little. Then with a shrug she hopped in, and with a leafy branch pulled Slub Glub on top of her. "I didn't know water can talk," she whispered to Slub Glub.

"Oh yes. Most bodies of water are good conversationalists. I knew a man who went so far as to get married to the sea, even."

Chapter 17

Strange Currents Carry Queer Cargo

47

Willowmina and Slub Glub bobbed along for thirty minutes or so, as the brook gently wound around various bends, getting a little wider as it got further along. "I feel some floaters upstream a ways, near my neck," the water gurgled up at them.

"Your neck? Where are we now?" Willowmina asked. Slub Glub was asleep, nestled comfortably between her branches.

"My armpit, can't you tell?" Indeed, there was a sharp right-angled bank along their left side. A little while later they passed by a trio of ghosts, who were being passively swept along by the current. Their eyes were rolled up towards the stars, and their legs were rigid as they buoyed past. "At least they're not too heavy, due to their missing various parts," the water reflected.

"You don't happen to know how they met their unfortunate ends, do you? I've got to keep them from

coming this way any more," Willowmina asked.

"Ah, you'd be doing both of us a favor if you did," the babbling brook replied. "They're really stinking up my scent. And I've found the stray eyeball or left arm dangling down in my muddy bottom. But no, I just roll them along, I don't know what their story is. But there may be a clue up ahead—I think I see one of their boats."

48

The brook was right; there was a small wooden raft appearing on the horizon, seemingly unoccupied. It looked like it had been in some bad situations; there were large holes in its sides and its deck was severely splintered. Willowmina rustled one of her branches on the head of the sleeping Slub Glub. "Wake up, blue thing, and find out what you can from that broken boat."

As the not-quite-a-life raft approached, Slub Glub dutifully latched onto its hull with one tentacle and pulled it alongside them. Peering over the edge, he spied some strange scrawls scratched into its sides. "There seem to be some drawings in here, scratched into the wood."

"Ah, maybe that's a clue, what do they look like?"

"There's some stick figures, and some things that maybe are supposed to be boats, and they're being turned upside down by a kind of giant black spider."

Chapter 18

Further Evidence
of Bad Times

50

"Ooooh, I don't like the sound of that," Willowmina shuddered.

"Yes, there are strange things in the deep sea, weird things best left in its briny depths," the babbling brook chimed in, unhelpfully.

"What else is in there?" Willowmina asked Slub Glub, who was still inspecting the battered lifeboat.

"Well, there's these," he said, holding up a tubular telescope in one hand and a pair of undergarments in the other.

"Bring back the telescope," Willowmina said, extending one of her branches towards her squat, blue companion so that he could climb back on top of her. Slub Glub, not knowing what a telescope was, dropped the cylindrical thing and made his way back carrying only the undergarments, which were silk and flowery. "No, no, those are bloomers. Bring back the

tube!" Willowmina instructed.

"That's mine," croaked a wretched voice. "Give it back, ye squalid landlubbers!" It was another ghost, who was now peering over the side of the little boat Slub Glub had just vacated.

"Oh, he was there too," Slub Glub commented to Willowmina.

52

"Ah, never mind, I don't need it where I'm goin' anyway," the ghost relented, his teeth falling out as he spoke, revealing gangrenous gums. A large hook jutted out uselessly from his shoulder, which was missing an arm.

"The Baron is just up the river, he'll take you to the next world," Willowmina told the ghost, trying to be helpful.

"And it's about time. This one's full of monsters," the deceased sailor shuddered. "Which you'll find out soon enough, if you keep goin' in that fool direction —that's where the Sea Devil lives, with its thousand spinning arms and unblinking soul-stealing eyes, and a mouth as big as the moon and twice as smelly!" he blathered, pointed his hook upstream.

Chapter 19

Sea of Strange

"Well, there's something fishy going on, and we've got to get to the bottom of it, so goodbye, good luck, and say hello to the Baron for us," Willowmina told the poor dead sailor.

"Ah yes, Baron Saturday, I'm comin' to ya," the sailor muttered, and he drifted down-river.

Slub Glub perched himself on Willowmina's trunk as they bobbed and weaved through the twists and turns of the babbling brook, which had widened into a stream, and then a river, and eventually became so large that it seemed to go on forever in all directions. "This is the end of the line for me, odd folks," the body of water babbled. "We're about to empty into the Big Drink, the Ocean of the Unknown. Watch out for the serpents and such," it said, and with a last gurgle fell silent. Willowmina and Slub Glub were alone and adrift on a puddle one thousand miles wide and a hundred miles deep.

53

A. Goldfarb

An uneventful hour passed of aimless floating on the ocean waves. "See if you can see anything in this sea," Willowmina said to Slub Glub. Since she was floating on her back, all she saw was sky.

Slub Glub fiddled with the telescope. "Hmm, nothing... No, nothing there... Oh, wait a minute. There we are."

"What is it?"

"Well, I think I see the soul-stealing eye that sailor was talking about."

Willowmina rotated herself so that she could see what Slub Glub was staring at, and found that the blue mutant's telescope was poking into the ocular orb of a mammoth creature, pink and slimy, with vast tentacles festooned with suction cups connected to a body the size of a mountain. "Ooooh," she said, very impressed. "Are you a god?" Willowmina asked the monster. In response, the great pink thing sprayed them both from head to toe with gallons of black ink.

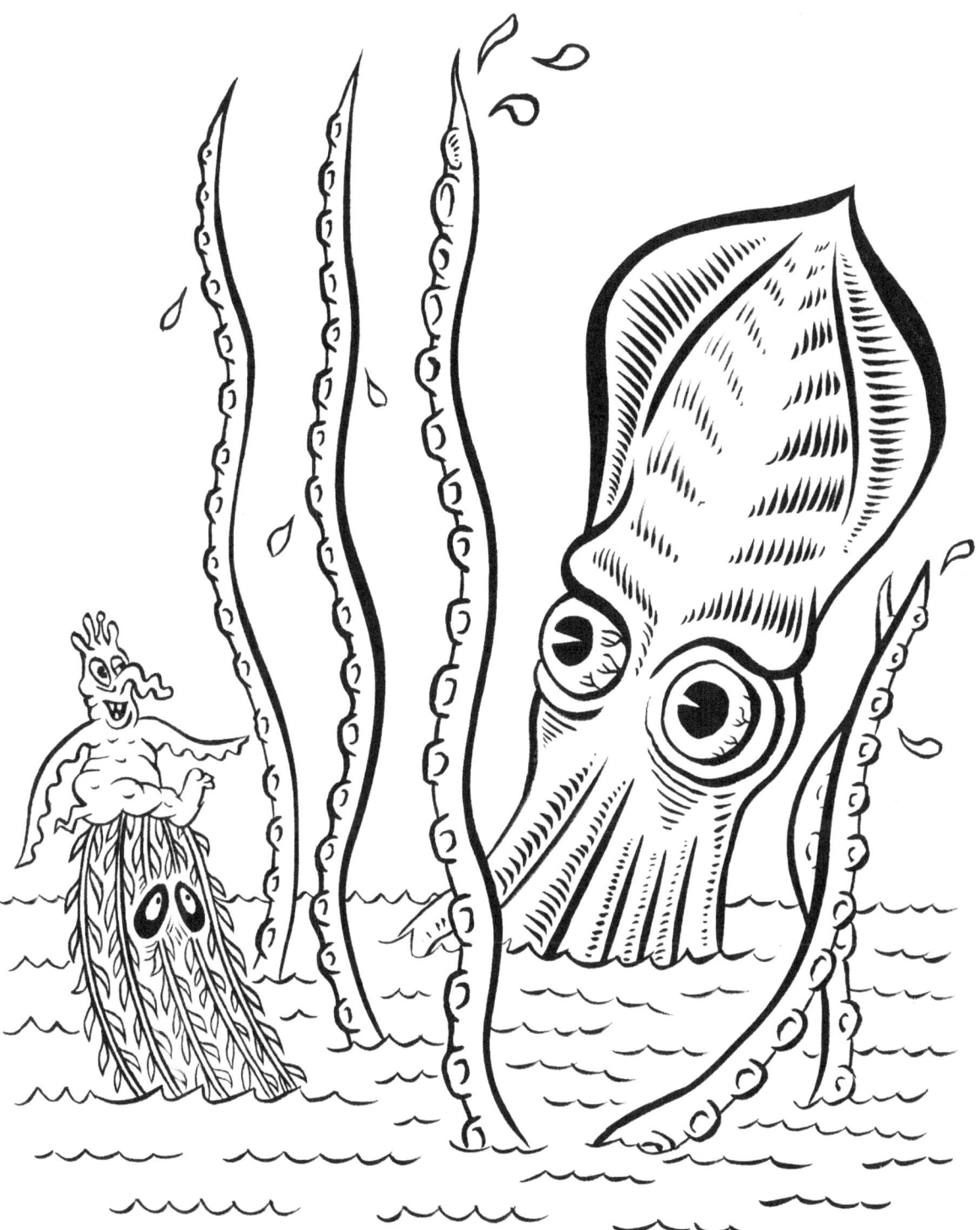

Chapter 20

Crab Caravan

56

And so there they were, Willowmina buoyed on the ocean waves and Slub Glub perched upon her branches, both now black as tar and covered in the dank sticky ink sprayed by the giant looming sea horror before them, who had now turned its attention elsewhere. Slub Glub and Willowmina found themselves similarly distracted, by an irritating nipping at their heels.

Slub Glub raised his foot, which had been dangling in the water. A crab was attached to it, its pointy pincers dug deep into his toes. "Aaaugh! It's a baby sea spider!" he screamed. "Why do things keep trying to eat me?" he moaned.

Willowmina, who was similarly afflicted, was shaking the crustaceans out of her leaves. "They're crabs," she said. "I wonder what they're doing this far out at sea?" Indeed, there were many crabs among them —so many that they formed a pink chain as far as the eye could see. While Willowmina and Slub Glub were trying desperately to shake these bothersome crabs off

Slub Glub in the Weird World of the Weeping Willows

of their bodies, the great pink tentacled ink-squirting monster-god of these worrisome waters, who was technically a giant squid, was engaged in a somewhat opposite activity. It was splashing furiously with its great gaping mouth wide open, ingesting and digesting these exoskeletal creatures.

In doing so, the huge squid created great tidal waves with its eight twirling tentacles, which had the unfortunate effect of drowning Slub Glub and Willowmina. "Glub Glub" was all Slub Glub could say as he found himself submerged in the briny depths of the endless ocean. As Willowmina also went deep below the black nefarious waters, she had the realization that this was how the ghost sailors must have died—they were drowned in the turbulent wake of the giant squid as it fed on crabs.

Chapter 21

Interrupted Underwater Slumbers

58

Slub Glub, who actually would have been able to swim if he had bothered to try, sank like a stone. As his lungs filled with seaweed, he turned an even darker shade of blue. He rested peacefully on the ocean floor, waiting for the long nap that would finally be his.

Up above, the giant squid (whose proper name was Seamort) was busy trying to swallow as many of the little pink pinching crabs as possible. The crabs seemed almost happy to oblige, offering little resistance as they surfed down the great gaping gullet of the monstrous leviathan. After several frenetic moments of swallowing, sucking and thrashing about, Seamort had eaten all the crabs around and let out a mighty belch.

It was then that something blue and strange caught Seamort's eye. That strange blue thing was Slub Glub, who lay at the bottom of the water below, his tentacles flopped among the coral crusts of the

ocean's briny bottom. Seeing Slub Glub's limp, noodly tentacles, similar to the squid's own, awakened some sort of familial paternal instinct in the massive pink squid's Squishy cephalopodic brain, and he dove down in Slub Glub's direction.

Seamort's giant pink tentacle reached through the ocean's dark depths towards Slub Glub, who thought this was the mighty finger of the Lord coming forth to nudge him to the afterlife. Slub Glub was surprised, then, to find the Great Squid's tentacle curl around him gently and pull him swiftly to the surface.

Emerging once again at the top of the water, and still cradled in Semort's twisting, suction cup-festooned appendage, Slub Glub stared at Seamort's slimy face and also registered a subconscious connection. Though they differed greatly in size and color, and Seamort had eight tentacles to Slub Glub's two, they appeared to be from the same general class of organism.

"Are you my mother?" Slub Glub asked.

59

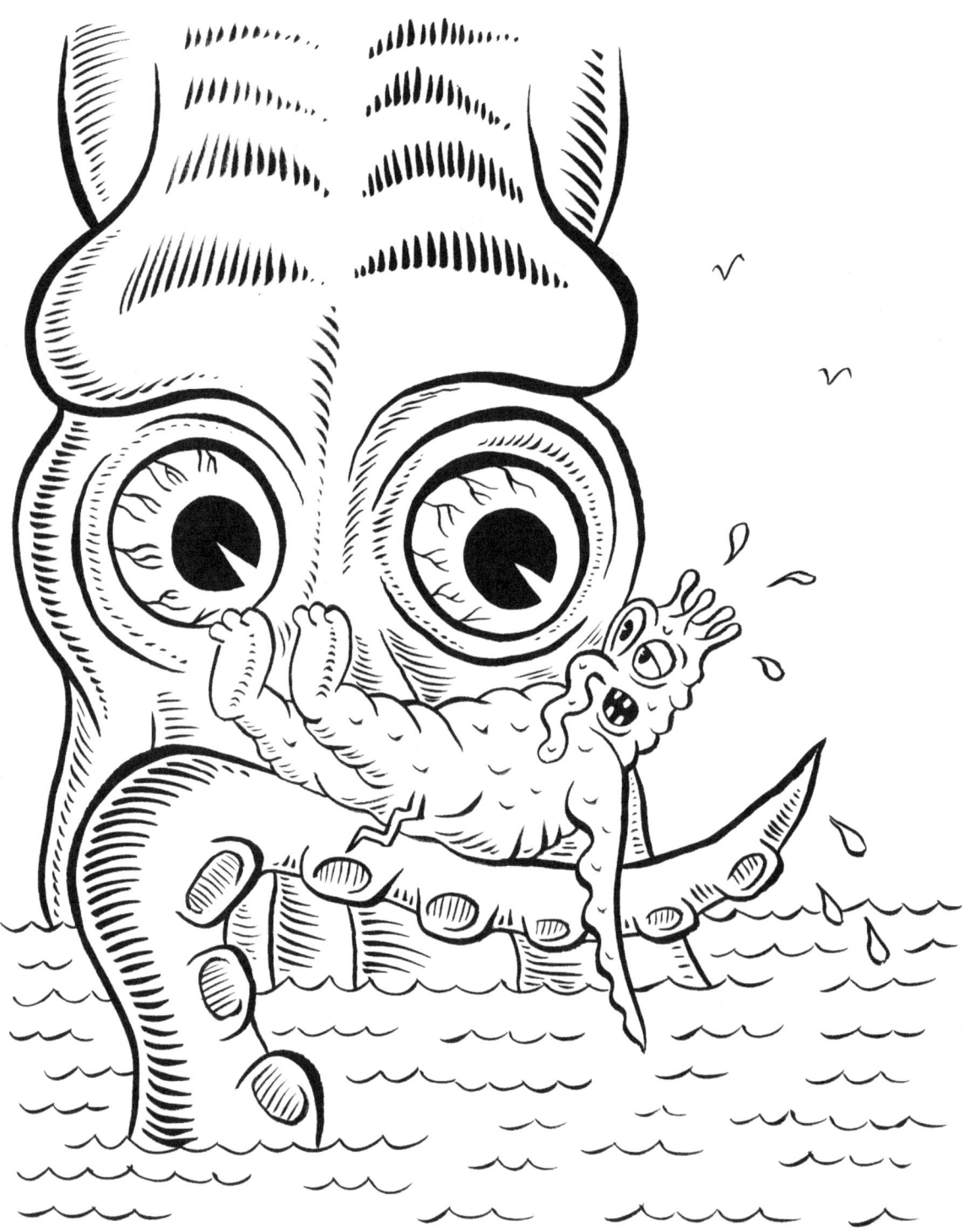

Chapter 22

Black Bathtub Beginnings

61

Seamort was not, in fact, Slub Glub's mother. Not only was Seamort a male giant squid, which at best would have made him Slub Glub's father, but Slub Glub had not been conceived by the usual method. Slub Glub was the product of man's nefarious ingenuity and nature's shiftless flexibility. He was born in a bathtub.

To be more specific, the chemical agents that acted as the catalyst for his unnatural life were mixed in a bathtub-like vessel within the Research and Development Laboratory of General National, a corporation of conglomerated concern of consolidated commercial enterprise. They were a big business, run by big business men, who did sinister things and made great gobs of money doing so. Their scientists were trying to discover a chemical ingredient that they could put in potato chips to make them taste like soda pop. The boss of General National, who always wore a four-piece suit, was convinced that if they could sell a bag of chips that

tastes like soda, it would sell as well as chips and soda combined, which would generate enough revenue for him to have his bones replaced with solid gold.

In pursuit of this noble goal, the dutiful white-coated scientists of the General National labs combined different ingredients in their bathtub to see if any would make potato chips taste like soda pop. On one fateful day, the ingredients in question were lemon juice and frog's fingers. It was then that the useless discovery was made that when lemon juice touches the fingers of a frog, it becomes a darkly-colored, sticky goo that smells like moldy fish lungs and stains all that it crosses with a permanent purplish-blackish tattoo. Repulsed, the scientists did what scientists who work at big corporations usually do, which is they flushed the horrible mess out a long tube and into the waters of the nearest stream.

62

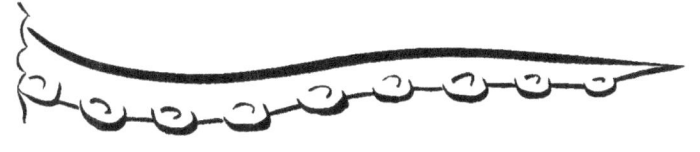

Chapter 23

Slub Glub's Birthday

It was a sunny June afternoon when the sludgy chemical refuse of the General National corporation exited from its long journey through rusty cylindrical tubes to its eventual home in the boggy creeks of the Lost Hills Nature Preserve, where it mingled with the more natural fluids that had come by way of rain and dewdrops.

A sizzling sound was heard as the black goop perverted the surface of the small lake that adjoined the creek, and the waters began to bubble and the fish swam away in fright. The woodland creatures gathered around in curiosity, observing the frothing waters of their newly polluted lake, which was washing strange bubbles onto the shore.

It was at this strange juncture in time that a human being arrived, carrying a squirming cephalopod in a plastic bag. This mousy individual looked furtively about, as the bag in his hand contained a small, angry octopus, which his daughter had purchased from an ad in the back of a comic book. His wife was disturbed

by the pet, and had demanded that this unfortunate man abandon the creature in the woods. Seeing the bubbling, sizzling lake, he emptied the octopus out of the bag and into the black oozing waters and scurried off to civilization.

64

As one might imagine, the chemically altered lake had unusual effects on the octopus and the natural order of things. When fall came, the octopus laid her eggs. The eggs were a strange blue color, and their mother rejected them, seeking a better life upstream. A group of possums stumbled across them, and took them for their own, because possums aren't terribly smart. Then one grey October morning the eggs hatched, and among the strange brood that emerged was Slub Glub, who came into the world a mutant creation, with yellow eyes and fevered mind.

Chapter 24

The
Monstrosity's Lament

65

But all of that was in the past. Getting back to the present situation, Slub Glub was raised above the water in the gentle curve of Seamort's massive pink tentacle. This was a good thing, for though Slub Glub, being semi-octopus in origin, was able to breathe underwater, he did not know that he could, and thus had not been trying to, and would surely have drowned. Seamort inspected Slub Glub carefully, and found him confusing.

At this point Willowmina bobbed back up to the surface. "I'm glad I'm made of wood," she sputtered. Then seeing that Seamort had stopped thrashing about and was holding Slub Glub aloft, she saw her opportunity to get some answers. "Hey! Big pink thing! You almost killed us, you know." Her earlier reverence for the giant squid had now turned to annoyance at nearly being drowned.

Seamort looked at her with surprise, as he hadn't noticed her before. "Oh, I'm so sorry," he said, surprisingly regretful. A tear even seemed to form in his giant eye.

Willowmina was a little ashamed at her harsh tone. "Um, no problem, I guess your mind was on those crabs."

"Those crabs! Those crabs will be the death of me!"

66

"The death of you? Don't you mean the death of them? And us, and all the sailors that get caught in your thrashing tentacles as you try to swallow all those crabs?"

"Don't you think I'd stop if I could?" Seamort wailed. "Look at me!" Slub Glub and Willowmina looked at him, but were unclear as to his meaning. "I'm huge!" he continued. "I've grown gigantic from eating so many crabs, and pink like them to boot."

"But aren't you a giant by nature?" Willowmina asked?

"Not like this. I would have some self respect, and eat a reasonable diet, if those deviled crabs weren't so tasty and plentiful."

Chapter 25

Crabby Complaints

68

"Okay, don't worry. All we'll have to do is convince the crabs to stop coming this way, and then you'll stop eating all of them, which means that no more sailors will be drowned by your great thrashing tentacles as you stuff them into your mouth, and therefore no more ghosts will be floating down the babbling brook on their way to be guided by Baron Samedi to the afterlife, and thus we'll have no more witches who think they're being haunted hypnotizing hyenas to create havoc, and as a result no more frightened raccoons hiding in and nibbling on willow tree leaves, causing us to cry and flood the forest, leading to sharks biting Slub Glub's rump," Willowmina expostulated. "Only problem is, there aren't any more crabs left to discuss this with, as you've eaten them all."

"It's all my fault," Seamort moaned, wiping his tears with Slub Glub's nose. "But more crabs will come, they always do." Just then, as if on cue, the first of a new wave of pink snapping crabs appeared, poking its pincers above the water. It was the first in a long line,

extending towards the distant horizon. Seamort got a glazed look in his giant eyes and began frothing at the mouth; his tentacles began to bristle, and it was clear that he was about to go into a renewed feeding frenzy. Willowmina shouted for him to stop.

"Wait! We must find out where they're coming from, and why!" she yelled, and Seamort snapped out of his trance, relaxing his eight great squid arms. Willowmina addressed the crab, who was pinching the bark of her trunk. "Little pink crab, why are you so far out to sea, in this dangerous place where as you can see you're about to be eaten by a giant squid?"

"Oh, what's the difference," the crab replied in a tiny, whiny voice. We can be eaten by a giant squid, or stepped on by oiled apes, or split in half by pointy planks of wood. All options end the same way."

69

Chapter 26

Ballad of the Sad Crab

70

Willowmina thought about this, and replied, "Hmmm. It sounds like you've had some trouble at home. Why don't you tell us about it."

The crab, now joined by a baker's dozen of his fellow crustaceans alongside him, then burst into sonnet.

"Oh once we were happy and free
And selfish in our shell-fish-ness
Thinking only of the surf and sea
And sands of golden grainy bliss

But strange pink monkeys from the trees
Grew smart and lost their hairs
Then they came to our golden shores
And sat tanning in their chairs

Plastic umbrellas darkened our skies
Children all building castles

Slub Glub in the Weird World
of the Weeping Willows

Flip-flops trampling our soft pink heads
A beach of endless hassles

And no salvation in salt water is found
Just sporting monkeys floating around
On boards that skate upon the surf
Crushing us for what it's worth

We will not go back on this or any day
In these bleak waters we shall decay
And fall into the flapping maw
Of tentacled squid with giant jaw"

71

"Pink monkeys? I've only seen brown ones," mused Slub Glub, once the chorus of crabs had completed their song of sorrow.

"Oh wait," Seamort chimed in. "Hairless pink monkeys? They must mean human beings."

"Human beings? What are those?" Willowmina inquired.

"They were children of the monkeys, but then they lost their hair and started wearing sandals and they do like to lounge around on beaches cooking in the sun, so I could see how that would get in the crabs' way."

"How do you know all this?"

"I read books," Seamort replied mysteriously, and then the frenzy came over him again and he began

diving after the crabs, who made no effort to get away as he swallowed them whole.

Willowmina grabbed Slub Glub by his knobby forehead and pulled him away from the tsunami of Seamort's thrashings as he fed. "You know what we have to do," she said to him.

"What's that?"

"We've got to find these human beings and keep them from driving these crabs into deep water."

72

Chapter 27

Across the Great Green Sea

73

Like lemmings lined up to jump off a cliff, the chain of crabs coming towards Seamort's insatiable appetite extended far back in a straight line across the ocean, so to get to the beach and find these hairless monkeys from which the crabs were fleeing, all Slub Glub and Willowmina had to do was follow the trail of crustaceans across the water. Willowmina floated alongside the line of crabs, while Slub Glub walked on top of them, hopping from one exoskeleton to the next.

Along the way they passed the ruins of ancient civilizations, which had sunk into the endless green depths eons ago. The curious spires of their long-lost houses of worship jutted out at crooked angles from below the sea's slimy surface; evidence of weird religions whose beliefs died with the flooding of their societies. Idols of forgotten gods lay rotting on the bed of the ocean below, fish and lichen swarming among them. Peering down, Slub Glub thought he saw a statue of a creature that looked very much like him, once the lord over an extinct race and

now an edifice eroding underwater, drowned with the citizens that once paid it tribute.

Eventually a shore emerged over the horizon, and Willowmina and Slub Glub saw their first glimpse of the human beings of which the crabs and Seamort had spoken.

74

Swollen pale creatures with mirrors over their eyes, these mammals rolled about in the dirt and set fire to meat. Some of them dodged jellyfish in waves, and others were buried up to their necks in sand. Slub Glub and Willowmina were filled with confusion and dread at the sight of them.

Chapter 28

Landlubbers

As they reached the sandy embankment, Slub Glub stepped off of the final crab in the chain of vacating crustaceans, and saw the reason for their massive pink exodus. The beach was fraught with danger. Human beings in garish-colored swim trunks were riding surfboards that collided with the ocean, each other, and all manner of sea creature. On the sandy beach there was a constant hubbub of people as they played strange games with nets and balls and engaged in oblique mating rituals involving strange lotions and awkward squawking. Children were re-shaping the surface of the dunes with sharp pails, further disrupting the peace and sending the small pink crabs scuttling for the deep water and their eventual squid-ish demise.

Slub Glub noticed a sedentary female of the species, seemingly comatose on a horizontal chair, smeared with glistening ointment. Slub Glub thought she might be someone's meal, as the always-angry sun

76

was turning her a golden brown, and the oils smeared across her seemed to hasten the process. Seeing a faint resemblance between this creature and himself, Slub Glub ventured forth to inquire what had brought everyone to this un-hospitable spot and to engage in such disruptive behavior.

"Excuse me," Slub Glub said tentatively. The creature's eyes were closed and it was making a fierce, rumbling, repetitive exhalation, which sounded like chainsaws. Slub Glub touched the thing's shoulder gently, then jumped back as it rumbled to life with a snort. The human squinted at Slub Glub.

"Be a dear and rub some more lotion on my back, will you?" it muttered, holding a bottle of ointment towards Slub Glub, whom it had mistaken for one of its children. Slub Glub peered into the bottle of lotion and was about to take a sip when Willowmina appeared and knocked it out of his hand.

"Don't drink that! We don't know, it might make us like them," she warned. "I hear the sound of a drum beating, let's go see if it's the Baron again."

Chapter 29

The Beat of Bongo Beach

78

The mysterious beats were the product of a set of bongo drums being pounded on by a young man attired in a black turtleneck and a scruffy goatee. He was entranced in his playing, oblivious to the approach of a willow tree and a globby blue mutant. Willowmina scratched him with her branch.

"Oh, wow. A tree - far out. And you're a freaky one, man," he said, seeing Slub Glub.

"Um, we're looking for answers," Willowmina said to him.

"Aren't we all, baby." He pointed the tip of his beret. "But the question is, what's the question?" He spoke in an odd syncopated lilt, thumping on his bongos with his palms as he prattled. Slub Glub and Willowmina looked at each other, befuddled. Beneath

his dark glasses, the young man stared into space.

"Are you a warlock?" Slub Glub asked him.

"Naw, man, I just come out here to dig those crazy waves and gaze at all the chicks. So what's your scene, hepcats? Lay it on me."

"We're trying to find out what all these human beings are doing here on this beach," Slub Glub explained.

"Oh, I hear ya, brother. These squares and their suburban hassles are the pits. It's gettin' so there ain't nowhere to crash without getting busted by the pigs."

79

Slub Glub looked around to see where these pigs were. Willowmina, frustrated by the young man's incomprehensible language, said, "We just need to keep them from crowding out the crabs."

"I know it, leafy. The Man is messing with the natural order of things. The whole cycle is out of whack. Mother Nature is getting angry."

"Yes! Exactly!" Willowmina exclaimed, excited that this weirdo human seemed to understand the dilemma. "But why? Why is all this happening?"

The beach-nik stopped playing his bongos, and pointing his finger into the air, said somberly, "You'll have to ask Him."

Chapter 30

Assaulted by Emissaries of the All-Powerful Entity Above

Slub Glub and Willowmina both looked up to where the oddball's finger was pointed, but saw only a grey, smoggy sky. "I don't see anything," Slub Glub remarked.

"Ain't that the truth, kittens. God is dead."

"God?" Willowmina inquired, unfamiliar with the concept.

"The Powers That Be. The Man Upstairs."

"He's dead?" Willowmina asked, crestfallen that they might have finally come close to the source of their problems, only to find the perpetrator deceased.

"Well, that's what the newspapers say."

"And this is all his doing?"

The beach-nik twirled his fingers mysteriously. "Ha. Deep, baby. You're spiritual. I can dig it."

"Um, how can we talk to this god?" Willowmina asked.

82

Right then a man and a woman emerged from a nearby sand dune and rushed to Willowmina's side, pushing the young man in the turtleneck sweater out of the way. Evidently they had been lurking surreptitiously, waiting for just such an opportunity. "We can help you, my child," the man said. He wore a tie and a button down shirt with slacks, somewhat overdressed for a day at the beach. His companion was a matronly lady in a yellow frock and caked layers of makeup. She put her arm around Slub Glub.

"Have you heard The Word, my son, about the Mystical Potentate of Time and Space?" she said to him.

"Would he be the one that brought these people to the beach, driving the crabs into the water, and so on and so on?" Willowmina interjected.

"Of course," the man said paternally to her. "He's responsible for all things."

"Then we've got to talk to him!" Willowmina said, and without a word the man and woman dragged her and Slub Glub away from the beach, and into the dark city streets.

Chapter 31

Among the True Believers

84

The sight of a mobile willow tree and a misshapen mutant did not register much reaction on any of the human beings in the city, as most were looking down at the crusty sidewalks upon which they hurriedly walked. The man in the tie and the made-up woman brought Slub Glub and Willowmina to a bleak, black building with strange curves, like the shell of a clam turned inside out. Tall men with concave bellies, draped in elaborate robes, were carved in stone around the sides. The windows displayed images of giant snakes curled around withering trees with skull-shaped fruit drooping from the boughs.

The man and woman pushed Slub Glub and Willowmina through a heavy wooden door and then stood behind them with arms folded. Inside, the building was somehow twice as large as it was outside, with a ceiling that rose up twelve stories into a sharp point, from which hung a massive idol of a headless man, devoid of clothing. Red

liquid poured out of multiple holes in the figure's body, gushing downward in a steady stream and into a set of silver goblets that were placed beneath this macabre fountain.

The only light was from flickering candles placed in alcoves that rimmed the perimeter of the halls, which was devoid of furniture except for 31 large metal spikes that sprouted from the stone floor. On each of these spikes, a figure in a purple robe was leaning, the sharp point of each giant nail poking a hole through the fabric of their garment in a mild impalement. Their bodies were covered so thoroughly by the ritual cloths that it was hard to tell if they were men or women.

85

"I think these folks are cannibals," Slub Glub whispered to Willowmina, who shuddered.

Chapter 32

The Creeping Ritual

87

A woman covered in sparkling white fabric emerged from a crevice in the corner. She raised her arms as if about to fly away, and screamed aloud the cryptic phrase "Arzoth Fu Ma'aloch."

"Arzoth Fu Ma'alock," the bent, hooded figures chanted back in unison, then rose up and stood in rows, all of them staring towards the weird old lady.

"Garuth Et Nyl'yark," she shouted, and again the assembled congregation (and Slub Glub as well, carried along by the heat of the moment) repeated the incantation. The worshippers then bent back onto their metal spikes, and the white lady pulled back the hood of her robe, revealing a large bronze medallion dangling over her forehead. She touched it with her claw-like fingers, and began to babble.

"Oh great fiery wheel, we pledge our personage to your effluvient largesse. What hideous finger looms beneath the surface of our daily crust, and what deliverance of truth and velveteen can absolve our frail

frolics, if not a mighty cannon from your eternal eye?"

She then took her place behind a pulpit that was located beneath a large mural of a three-headed cow being ridden by a purple man with great gobs of cottony hair. The priestess took a large book into her hands, and opened the musty tome to read. "In the year 4243, the first cleavage of the ground was visited untoward the peoples verily..."

89

Willowmina had sensed immediately that this was no place to be. Unfortunately, the white-shirted man and yellow-dressed woman who had brought them there were guarding the door to block their exit. However, Willowmina had been slowly growing her dangling vines around their feet during the ceremony, and when the leader of the cult produced a large gong and struck it with a bone, producing a mind-numbing ring, Willowmina seized the opportunity to contract her vines gently, sliding the guards, who were hypnotized by the words of the priestess, away from the door. She quickly scurried out the door, but had to return to fetch Slub Glub, who now wanted to join the order permanently. After she shook him upside down he thought better of it, and they made a hasty exit down the steps of the cathedral and ran across the street.

Chapter 33

The Man with the Lampshade Hands

90

Willowmina and Slub Glub came to a rest at a park down the street from the weird church, uncertain how to proceed. "That was no help at all," Willomina said, feeling low.

In a similar state, but smellier, was a man with knotted hair and dressed in a garbage bag. He wheeled his shopping cart up alongside them. The cart was filled with an untidy collection of lampshades and Chinese newspapers, and strapped together with duct tape. The occasional broom handles stuck out of this mound of refuse, and a number of doll heads were affixed to the ends of the broomsticks.

He took two ratty lampshades out of his collection and sat down on a bench next to Slub Glub and Willowmina. Placing one over each hand, he waved his arms and conducted a conversation between the two light coverings.

"It's autumn and the piano music has stopped

playing," he mumbled out of the side of his mouth as he shook the pink and orange lampshade that was on his right hand. "When a letter arrives from acquaintances upstate, an ill wind will blow down shortly after," he drooled out of the other side of his mouth, gesturing with a shredded wicker shade on his left appendage.

The man was silent for a moment, then suddenly exclaimed, "Will you two shut up!" and he threw the two lampshades off his hands and into the street. He then turned to Slub Glub and Willowmina and asked, "Do you believe them?"

"Not particularly," Willowmina responded, not being familiar enough with humanity to judge whether the man's behavior was odd; based on recent experiences at the beach and in the temple, this was par for the course.

"That's what I thought," he said, tugging on a lock of his hair that dangled over his nose and was tied in a greasy knot with a small green ribbon. "So what brings you two to this desolate stretch of the city?" he asked.

"Well..." Willowmina took a deep breath. Slub Glub then put his tentacle out to stop her, saying, "I'll do it this time."

Chapter 34

Collect Calls to Heaven

"I was being bitten by sharks which had swum inland when Willowmina and her family had been crying so much that their tears made a puddle that stretched to the ocean, but they were only crying because raccoons were nibbling on their leaves at night and making them bald in patches, but it turns out that they were only doing that because they were hiding from the hyenas and got hungry. The hyenas were scaring the raccoons because the witches had hypnotized the hyenas to go around cackling at people. The witches' intent had nothing to do with raccoons, though, they were just hoping to keep the ghosts at bay; ghosts that they thought they'd accidentally brought back from the dead with their spells. In fact, the ghosts were just passing through on their way to the next life, as they had been drowned by the tentacles of a giant squid as it feasted on crabs. These crabs were only coming near the giant squid to escape the crazy human beings on the

94

beach. But as for why the crazy human beings are on the beach, and therefore making everything else happen as it does, apparently that's a question that only The Man Upstairs can answer, according to the fellow with a drum we met at the beach, which is why we went to that building across the street but the Upstairs Man was missing his head and wasn't talking."

"I see," the vagrant replied, pondering Slub Glub's lengthy explanation, which had been delivered hurriedly in a single breath. "No, he wouldn't be found across the street," the man with the lampshades said. He stared into space for a while, and then brightened as he realized the solution. "I know, you can call him on the telephone!"

"What's that?" Willowmina asked. Slub Glub had walked over to the lampshades that the man had thrown, and had put them on his tentacles, but couldn't get them to talk. The derelict walked over to his shopping cart and rummaged around, eventually pulling out two coffee cans with a string attached. He took one can and placed it in a pile of dirt over to their left, and gave the other can to Willowmina. "Go ahead," he said.

Willowmina took it in her branch. "How do I use it?" she asked.

"Just talk into it, and ask for the Omnipotent Master of All Reality."

Chapter 35

Communications with Lord Lump-Lump

96

Although technically neither of them had ears, Slub Glub creeped up next to Willowmina and put his head against the coffee can as well. "Hello?" Willowmina asked tentatively into the tin, where remains of coffee grounds still resided.

To their surprise, the can in the dirt at the other end of the string rang with an electronic bell-like sound. The vagrant picked up the other end, brushed his tangled hair back, and then spoke into the receiver. "Hello," he said. His voice was now completely different; it was strong and authoritative, without a trace of the drool-ish muttering he'd exhibited earlier. Also, there was a resounding echo to the sound of it, as if he was speaking from atop a mountain. "What can I do for you?"

"Is this the Omnipotent Master of All Reality?" Willowmina asked.

"People call me by many names. You," he said with emphasis, "can call me Lump-Lump." Neither Slub Glub

nor Willowmina were looking at the man as he spoke into the other end, but if they had they would have seen that his face had transformed—whereas previously he had been squinty and riddled with tics, his eyes were now wide-open and shined with a strange glow, and his jaw had straightened.

Slub Glub wiggled his mouth towards the opening of the can, which was difficult, since his nose was warty and dangling. "Mr. Lump-Lump, my name is Slub Glub, and we were hoping to receive from you an explanation for a series of circumstances that we've recently experienced, and perhaps a method that we could employ to avoid this chain of events in the future, so that we might be free from certain inconveniences we're now experiencing." Willowmina shook a little in her branches, surprised by Slub Glub's sophisticated speech. Apparently talking to God was improving his diction.

97

"Go on," the man said.

"Well, you see, I was being bitten by sharks which had swum inland when Willowmina and her family had been crying so much that their tears..."

"Stop," Lump-Lump said through the can. "I understand your problem."

"But I haven't finished..." Slub Glub started to say.

"I am the Omnipotent Master of All Reality and I know all things," he said, sounding matter-of-fact rather

than boastful. "Tell me, what planet is this that you're calling from."

Slub Glub wasn't too sure, but Willowmina leaned forward. "Earth," she said.

"Ah, there's the problem," said Lump-Lump.

98

Chapter 36

The Miscreation Story, Part One

99

Slub Glub and Willowmina looked quizzically into the tin cup telephone and breathed in a faint aroma of instant coffee. At the other end of the connecting string, the man with the knotty hair was standing very straight, his newly-excellent posture straining the confines of the garbage bag he was wearing. In his resonant voice, he spoke at length:

"Yes, Earth, that is a problem.

"Earth, I'm afraid, does not work exactly as planned. And the reason for that is simple. I was not its creator. But I was its planner.

"It was a long, long, long, long time ago. The heavens were in place, the cosmos was unfurling, and it was time to give life to a planet. I had created worlds before, but they were only simple spheres of rock and mist and the occasional fungus; nothing that I was terribly proud of. I envisioned something much grander, a shining jewel in space, which would be home to countless creeping things.

There would be species of all stripes, carefully engineered to fit together in perfect harmony, working in unison like maggots upon a corpse.

"After much laborious meditation, elaborate blueprints were drafted, in my own pen from a well of eternal ink, and drawn onto umpteen scrolls of the finest firmament. Once finished, having inscribed nearly every detail, I took a well-deserved repose. When I awoke, to my shock, I found that the scrolls were gone."

100

Chapter 37

The Miscreation Story, Part Two

101

"The culprits were some of my own angels, who had come across the blueprints while I was asleep and thought that these were instructions for them to follow. They meant well, but creating worlds is not for the novice, and as detailed as my plans were, there was no way that that they could understand how to properly assemble such a complicated construction. This was compounded by the fact that in a misguided attempt to please me, they worked in a hurry, hoping to have the Earth finished and ready by the time I awoke, as a surprise.

"Well, I was surprised all right, but not pleased. As you might imagine, I was unhappy about their having jumped the gun and built something that only I knew how to do properly. But what was done was done, and as the Earth was now in existence and contained life, there was no going back. The angels had gotten it partly

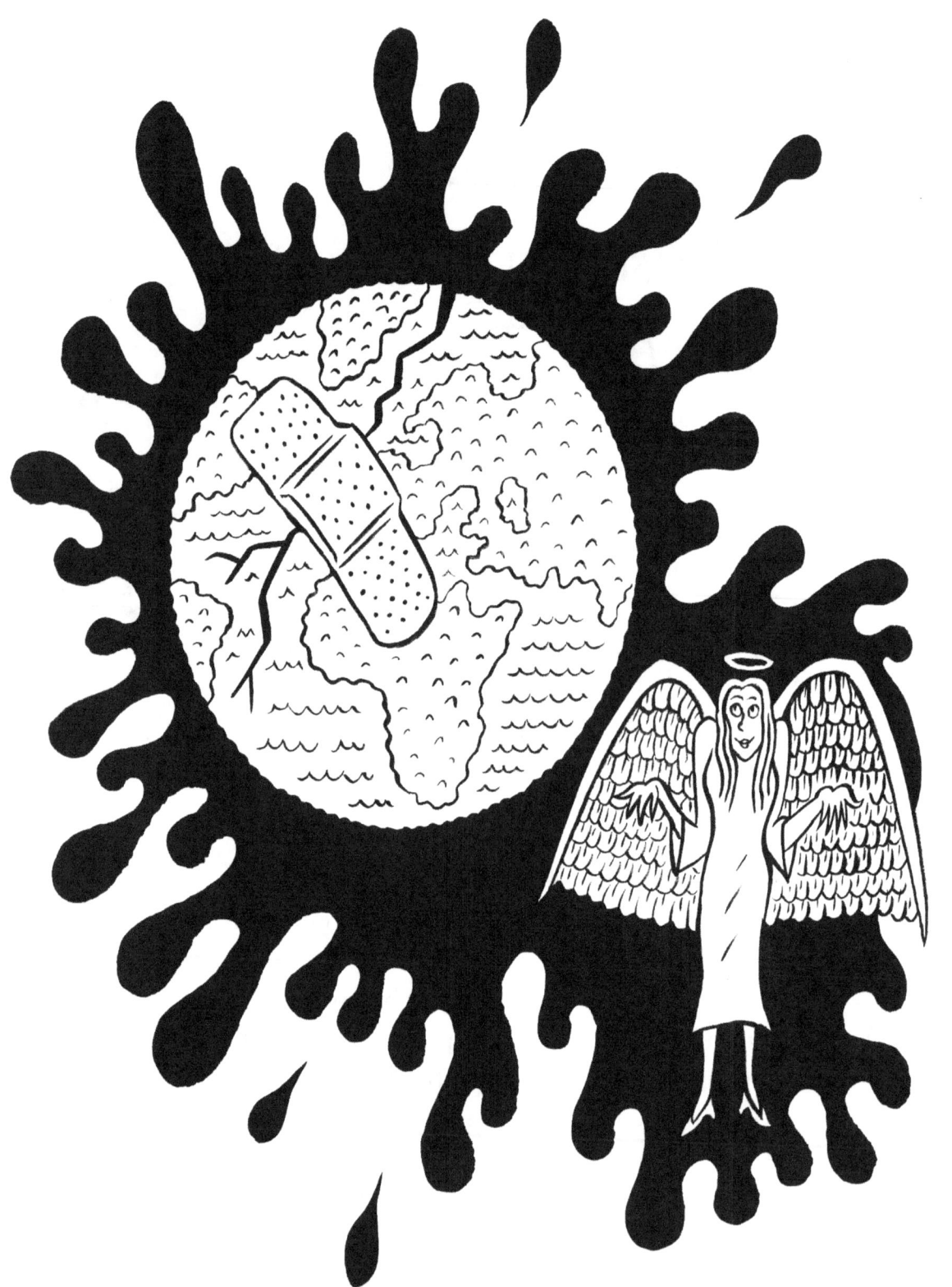

right; the world they made certainly contained a spark of my divine intent, which is only natural, as it was my plans that they were following, but as the angels are not Omnipotent Masters of All Reality, they of course got quite a bit wrong. As time progressed, these design flaws in the planet and its inhabitants only became more obvious. I checked in frequently to see how things were coming along on your world, and I even made a few attempts to fix things, but whenever I did it seemed to cause more harm than good. So I just let it be, and it turned out that the Earth had been created in a close enough fashion to my original plans that it pretty much works. At the least, if follows its own internal logic... But in short, your Earth was a mistake."

103

This seemed to conclude the stranger's story, and Willowmina asked, "What parts of the Earth don't work the way you meant them too?"

"Well, just about everything is slightly off," Lump-Lump answered through the homeless man with the coffee can next to his mouth. "For example, the raccoons weren't supposed to nibble on any branches, even if they were scared by hyenas. In my original plans, no living thing ingested another living thing. The fact that they do so on your world is just a by-product of my angels having put the cycle of life in the wrong-sized circle."

Chapter 38

Picking a Planet

104

"That must be a terrible disappointment to you," Willowmina responded.

"Oh, it was, but eventually I went ahead and created my world as I had intended it, and it worked out just as planned. The angels were quite embarrassed when they saw the difference between the two planets."

There were a few minutes of silence, and then Lump-Lump asked, "Does that answer your question?"

Willowmina sat and rustled her branches a little bit, thinking this all over. On one hand it was nice to have an explanation for all the misfortune they'd encountered, even if the explanation was only that everything on Earth is a mistake. On the other hand, that didn't provide much of a solution to the problem of the raccoons and everything else. "So," she said, "Just to clarify, on this other world you've made, the correct one, no raccoons would ever nibble on my leaves?"

"None of the problems of Earth are present in the world that I created as intended."

"Could we live there instead of on Earth?"

Slub Glub in the Weird World of the Weeping Willows

"Yes, all things are possible," Lump-Lump answered. "However, I must warn you, it is very different from the planet that you know."

"How different?"

"Very."

Willowmina and Slub Glub looked at each other. Willowmina shook her head full of leaves back and forth and put her branch on Slub Glub's tentacle. "I'm not going to go. I'll stay here, for better or worse. It's our world, even if it's not quite right."

Slub Glub thought for a moment, then put his mouth into the coffee can. "Oh mighty Lump-Lump, tell me, in this other world, would sharks still be biting on my bottom, and would the sun with its thousand angry arms roust me from my slumber too early in the morning?"

"None of the problems of Earth are present in the world that I created as intended," the deep voice repeated matter-of-factly.

"Then I want to live there!" Slub Glub exclaimed.

YES

Chapter 39

Let Go of the Earth

106

The derelict man put down his coffee can, and walked over to Slub Glub. He remained physically transformed from the stooped and babbling bum he had been; he walked with a straight back and continued speaking in the deep echoing voice of Lord Lump-Lump as he bent towards Slub Glub and said, "Prepare thyself, and I will send you there forthwith."

Slub Glub turned to Willowmina and hugged her drooping branches. "Goodbye, Willowmina, I must explore new horizons free of annoying mornings."

"Good luck to you, little blue thing. I'll be heading home now." She shuffled off the park bench and headed back in the direction they'd come from, to the beach, the ocean, the babbling brook, and eventually back to the forest and her grove of trees.

"Are you ready?" the man with the shopping cart asked, his eyes glowing.

"Let's go!" Slub Glub said, flailing his tentacles, as the sky suddenly went dark and the pavement around

them melted into a cascade of melting colors, like paint
going down a drain, or poop into a toilet. He had the
sensation of falling, and this continued for quite a while,
until Slub Glub grew bored and went to sleep.

107

Chapter 40

The New World

108

Slub Glub awoke after a long sleep, and when he opened his eyes, he found that he was no longer falling. He was on smooth, hard ground, and he yawned and stretched, then opened his eyes. What he saw was only more smooth, hard ground, extending in every direction for as far as his two yellow eyes could see. There was nothing but a great expanse of brown nothingness. Overhead, the sky was a pale blue, as the sun sat muffled behind a cloud, hanging in a state of twilight. "Well, at least it's peaceful here," Slub Glub said to himself, and then went back to sleep.

A little while later, having awoken from his nap, he decided to go exploring in his new home. He started walking, and walked for quite a while. There was nothing here, however; just endless smooth ground beneath a cloudy sky. No sounds, and no life, so far as he could see. Slub Glub started to get tired, and sat down, talking to himself. "I wonder why there's nothing around, except this very smooth ground?"

Slub Glub in the Weird World
of the Weeping Willows

As if in answer to his question, some green figures appeared on the horizon, moving towards him rather quickly. As they got closer, Slub Glub could see that they were trees. In fact, they were willow trees. "Oh, maybe Willowmina decided to come here after all?" he wondered, but soon realized that these willow trees were much bigger than Willowmina or the other ones back on Earth; they had great drooping branches, full of green leaves, which draped across the ground, kicking up clouds of dust as they whisked forward.

109

There were three of these great towering willows, and they didn't even notice Slub Glub as they skimmed past, and he had to jump to the side, or he would have been flattened by their branches as they scraped along the surface of the ground. He watched as they scurried off into the distance.

And that is when Slub Glub understood.

"Aha! The ground is smooth because these extra-long willow branches are sweeping it clean. And the reason the branches are so long and leafy is because no raccoons are nibbling on them, keeping them short. And therefore, nothing else is here but some fast-moving trees and some very smooth ground, as the willows are wiping the planet so clean that nothing else grows or lives."

Satisfied at having figured this out, Slub Glub sat down and did nothing for a while. Every half hour or so he saw some of the giant willow trees whiz by again.

Slub Glub in the Weird World
of the Weeping Willows

Soon, he was as bored as he'd ever been. "This planet may be peaceful, but it sure is dull," he thought. But he had an idea.

Slub Glub waited for the next willow to pass by, and when it did, he grabbed on to one of the branches as it passed and climbed upwards on the fast-moving tree. The willow was so large that it didn't even notice that Slub Glub was climbing on it, until Slub Glub took a large bite from one of its leaves.

Then it stopped moving, and started crying.

"Ouch! Why did you do that?" the willow tree asked, now noticing that there was a strange, small blue creature perched in its foliage, nibbling at it.

111

"I'm sorry, but with no reason to weep, all you do is sweep," Slub Glub said. "And there should be more to life than that."

The willow tree, having never seen a blue mutant before, and never having cried before, had no response to this, and continued to blubber. As its tears fell, the ground softened beneath them. "Now watch what happens," Slub Glub said, pointing to the ground below the willow's roots, which was made muddy by the pool of tears.

Weeds were starting to grow in the mud; new life was coming into being. Slub Glub had disrupted the harmony of this planet and tilted its balance, and soon all would be right, or rather wrong, in the new world.

the end

About the Author

Andrew Goldfarb resides in San Francisco, where he draws the long-running underground comic strip "Ogner Stump's One Thousand Sorrows," which tells of the trials and tribulations of everyman Ogner Stump and his blue mutant sidekick Slub Glub. He also travels the country performing as a one-man-surrealistic-rock-and-roll-band under the name "The Slow Poisoner." A patent medicine salesman, his Genuine Slow Poisoner Miracle Tonic is proven effective in the treatment of Elephantiasis, Cholera, Barnacles, Boils, The Fits, Excessive Abscesses, Necrosis, Lavender Fever, General Wasting, Consumption, Women's Troubles, Gout, Neuralgia, Wandering Limbs, Stoutness, Onanism and Disinterested Bladder. This is his second prose book, following "The Ballad of a Slow Poisoner," which was published by Eraserhead Press in 2007. He will plunge to his death over Niagara Falls in 2068.

www.ingramcontent.com/pod-product-compliance
Lightning Source LLC
Chambersburg PA
CBHW080841250626
47161CB00009B/3146